Samuel French Acting Edition

Delval Divas

by Barbara Pease Weber

SAMUELFRENCH.COM   SAMUELFRENCH.CO.UK

FOR PRODUCTION ENQUIRIES

UNITED STATES AND CANADA
Info@SamuelFrench.com
1-866-598-8449

UNITED KINGDOM AND EUROPE
Plays@SamuelFrench.co.uk
020-7255-4302

Each title is subject to availability from Samuel French, depending upon country of performance. Please be aware that *DELVAL DIVAS* may not be licensed by Samuel French in your territory. Professional and amateur producers should contact the nearest Samuel French office or licensing partner to verify availability.

For John, Ashley and Amy with all my love; for Bill and Paul with sincere thanks; for Dee, Carol, J.J., Susan, Bonnie Kelly, Diane and Nancy with gratitude for being friends and divas.

DELVAL DIVAS premiered at The Old Academy in Philadelphia, Pennsylvania in September, 2003, under the direction of William Peterson and Paul Muscarella with the following cast:

LUCILLE	J.J. Johnson
BETH ZIEGLER	Bonnie Kapenstein
ROSEMARY ADAMS	Carol Veach
STELLA WILD	Dolores Watson
LINDA ROBERTSON	Susan Lonker
SHARON WATSON	Kelly Melcher

THE DIVAS

STELLA WILD, MBA............over 40. Stockbroker convicted of insider trading. Made millions on Wall Street. Her assets are safely hidden in offshore accounts until the time comes when she can, once again, enjoy them. Stella is the "unofficial" boss or "Diva-in-charge."

ROSEMARY ADAMS, Esq.......over 40. Banking lawyer/Former Bank VP. JD/MBA in Finance. Convicted of skimmed and reallocated mortgage funds; well invested in property and offshore accounts. Rosie, brilliant in her own right, is the kind hearted and "compassionate "Diva."

LINDA ROBERTSON, M.D., Ph.D.................over 40. MD and former Senior Vice President of Fielweil HMO. Convicted of defrauding Medicaid in managed care scandal. Formerly a world-renowned cardiologist, Linda is the "neurotic Diva."

BETH ZIEGLER, MBA...............early to mid 30's. Information technology wizard. Convicted of internet/mail fraud. Sold commodities that didn't exist via internet and made a fortune. She has come to the end of her sentence. Beth is the calm, cool and collected "Diva."

LUCILLE.........30-40. Prison guard by day; MBA student by night. The Delval Divas, her friends and mentors, have provided Lucille with the confidence she needs to succeed in life. Lucille is the "Diva with the attitude." She has a tough and gutsy exterior but a tender interior.

SHARON WATSON....................late 20's-early 30's. Hairdresser. Arrested and charged with killing her ex-husband's third wife. Sharon resembles a "slightly younger" and "plainer" version of Beth. She is timid and not nearly as "worldly" as the other divas. Sharon is the sweet, nice and "innocent" Diva.

SYNOPSIS

Stella Wild, MBA, Rosemary Adams, JD, MBA, Linda Robertson, M.D., Ph.D., and Beth Ziegler, MBA, have quite a few things in common. Besides being educated, successful, professional women, they also share the same address. It isn't a swanky high rise apartment building or a beachfront condominium. Rather, they reside at the Delaware Valley Federal Correctional Facility, a low level security prison for white and "pink" collar criminals.

With the Warden in one pocket and their Corrections Officer in another, these Divas continue to indulge their lavish and luxurious lifestyles in "prison paradise". That is, until Beth is prematurely released (against her wishes) and the Divas, to their horror and dismay, are forced to room with a murderess. Adding insult to injury the Department of Corrections has announced its intention to close the Delval facility due to mismanagement and relocate inmates to the less than glamorous Black Rock Federal Prison.

Find out how the Divas save Delval, solve a murder and reunite on a Roman holiday. Who said that crime doesn't pay?

(LIGHTING SUGGESTION: The set is dark as to Beth's and Linda's cell as it is with respect to Stella and Rosemary's cell. When the lights eventually come up, we see that they are not "ordinary" cells at all. Rather, they are decorated and furnished quite lavishly—in a way quite opposite of what one would expect to find in a prison.)

DELVAL DIVAS

Act I – Scene 1

(SETTING: Cell Block A of the Delaware Valley Federal Correctional Institution, a low-level security prison for white and "pink" collar criminals.)

(AT RISE: Set is dark and as the curtain opens we hear the low, sad weeping of BETH who is seated alone in her cell. Spotlight comes up on BETH's distraught face. We hear the footsteps of LUCILLE, Guard, as she enters from Stage Left. LUCILLE stops, takes a deep breath, and enters BETH's cell. It would appear that BETH is being readied for her death sentence to be carried out. In reality, though, she is being released.)

LUCILLE. It's time.

BETH. No, not yet. It can't be.

LUCILLE. I'm sorry, Beth. Your time is up.

BETH. Please, I'm not ready.

LUCILLE. You'll never be ready, Beth. It's time to face the music. I have to take you now. I'm sorry.

(BETH cries.)

BETH. It's not fair! Why me? It's not my time!

(We hear LUCILLE taking the lid off of BETH's food tray.)

LUCILLE.   Look at this. I'm disappointed. You didn't touch any of your last meal. These are all of your favorites. What a waste. *(SHE replaces lid with a "clank".)*

BETH.   *(Tearfully)*   How can I think about eating at a time like this!

> *(At this point we hear the others from the next cell but still cannot see them in the darkness.)*

ROSEMARY.   Lucille, you heartless beast, give her five more minutes. Come on!

STELLA.   Yeah, what's wrong with you? Can't you see the girl is grieving? Think of yourself in her position.

LUCILLE.   I'll never be in her position.

LINDA.   Come on, Lucille, have some heart here. Where is your compassion?

ROSEMARY.   *(To BETH)*   We'll be right with you in spirit, honey. Just remember that.

LINDA.   If I could, I'd take your place, you know that, right? You don't deserve this. I'm so, so sorry.

STELLA.   Be brave, Beth. Be brave. Show them that you are going out with integrity, dignity and your head held high.

ROSEMARY.   *(Her composure cracking)*   Oh, Beth, I'll miss you so much. *(SHE weeps)*

LUCILLE.   All right! Now that's enough! You're making things worse than they already are. Quiet down in there! She's upset enough as it is without hearing you blubber. Save the tears for when it's your turn. Let's go. NOW Beth.

BETH.   No, please not yet, I can't…

LUCILLE.   *(To BETH.)*   If you don't cooperate with me, Beth, I'm going to have to call reinforcements and that won't be pretty. Is that what you want? Do you want to be dragged away kicking and screaming with your hands cuffed behind your back by two very large and menacing guards?

> *(BETH raises an eyebrow and gives facial expression*
> *as if to suggest that she may consider this type of man-*
> *handling to be kind of fun and kinky.)*

LUCILLE. Or, do you want get this over with quickly and quietly with me? Your choice, Beth. It's over now. Face it.

BETH. You can't do this to me!

LUCILLE. I'm not doing anything to you. You did it to yourself, remember?

BETH. I'm a model prisoner. Why are they doing this to me. Why won't the Governor reconsider? I want my lawyer. Where is my lawyer? There's still time for the Governor to reconsider, isn't there? What about the Warden? Why can't someone help me?

LUCILLE. It's too late, Beth. The Governor can't help you. Your lawyer can't help you anymore. The Warden can't help you anymore. They have done all they can do. This is it. LET'S GO!

> *(LUCILLE gently takes BETH's arm and pulls*
> *her to a standing position. The lights come up and we*
> *see that BETH is dressed fashionably for the street*
> *and carries a large suitcase-on-wheels in addition to a*
> *smart handbag and a laptop case.)*

BETH. This isn't fair. I don't want to go. I don't deserve to go. I haven't finished serving my sentence!

LUCILLE. I already explained this to you. The Review Board looked at your record again and decided it was time for you to go. They skipped over you twice in the last 12 months— at your own request, remember?

BETH. Well, they are making a huge mistake! I still have at least 14 more months in here the way I calculate it.

ROSEMARY. We'll e-mail you every day, honey. You know that. You'll be fine. Take that Hawaiian vacation we've been talking about. It'll do you good. I can make your travel arrangements on-line this afternoon if you want me to.

LINDA. *(As an authority, lecturing)* Don't forget your sunscreen. According to an article in last month's Journal of the American Medical Association, there is a statistically significant rise in the occurrence of malignant melanoma in women with your demographic profile that is linked to your generation's utter failure to adequately protect yourselves from the sun's ultraviolet rays. Remember! Sunscreen! At least SPF 30-45 if you can get it!

BETH. I don't want to go to Hawaii! I've been there a dozen times. There's nothing there but sunshine, sandy beaches and blue ocean. I want to stay here with all of you—where I don't NEED sunscreen. How will I ever get along by myself? You are all staying here. This is where I want to be, too. This is my life now. I can't ever remember a time in my life when I've been this comfortable and content.

STELLA. I know, I know, honey. We all feel that way too. But, you've got to be strong now. Plus, you can visit us twice a month you know and e-mail us every day!

BETH. That's not the same thing, Stella, and you know it.

LINDA. I'll never have another roommate like you, Beth. I want you to know that, from the bottom of my heart.

LUCILLE. Okay, that's enough. Come on, Beth. Your limo has been outside for half and hour already and the driver wants to know if you are coming or not.

BETH. He can wait, Lucille. He works for me, remember? This is more important.

> *(BETH enters the adjoining cell where STELLA,
> ROSEMARY and LINDA are gathered. Hugs,
> kisses and goodbye's all around. BETH straightens
> her jacket, holds up her head, and exits stage right.
> LUCILLE is left dragging BETH's suitcase(s) on
> wheels behind her.)*

4

STELLA. *(Picking up Wall Street Journal and opening it to stock page)* Poor kid. I really feel bad for her. I knew it would be a tough morning but I didn't think it would be this tough. Hey, look at this, MicroDynamics fell two points and TeqDotCom stopped trading. I wonder what's going on. *(To* **ROSEMARY***)* Quick, bring up the computer.

> *(***ROSEMARY*** goes to computer (or laptop) and punches in some code to get to the Dow Jones screen).*

ROSEMARY. Well, things could be worse, I guess. It could be one of us leaving. At least Beth has only been with us for a couple of years. She didn't really have time to get that acclimated.

LINDA. No? I think she acclimated herself in the first week! She was a super suite-mate. Not messy, kept to her side of the room, didn't smoke, funny, smart, articulate.

STELLA. Face it, she's one of us. I'll miss the hell out of her.

LINDA AND **ROSEMARY.** Me too.

> *(***ROSEMARY*** gets up and goes into cell formerly also occupied by* **BETH***)*

ROSEMARY. I'm starved. With all of the commotion about Beth leaving this morning we forgot to have breakfast.

> *(SHE removes lid to* **BETH***'s breakfast tray.)*

Yuck. Plain yogurt, granola and grapefruit. *(To* **STELLA** *and* **LINDA***)* I ask you, if you were going to have a "last breakfast" would you go low cal? Not me, the day they kick me out of this place I'm ordering bacon, sausage, home fries, a cheese omelet and chocolate-chip pancakes.

5

STELLA.   What are you talking about? You eat like that every day. No wonder all of your clothes are tight.

> *(Alternative dialogue if* **ROSEMARY** *is played by a thin actress: "What are you talking about? No wonder you have such incredible gas.")*

LINDA.   As your physician, I'm obliged to inform you, Rosemary, that your arteries are clogging as rapidly as the toilets did when I first checked in to this "resort" eight years ago. That reminds me—we have to tell Lucille to call the plumber to repair the broken jet on our Jacuzzi.

ROSEMARY.   *(Laughs and eating the breakfast that* **BETH** *didn't touch)* So what? In my "other life" I'd be concerned. Now I just enjoy myself and wear a larger size. Besides, nobody sees me in the Jacuzzi except you gals and I couldn't care less if you see my cellulite—as if you don't have any yourself, Linda!

> *(Alternative language if* **ROSEMARY** *is played by a thin actress. "So what? In my "other life" I'd be concerned. Besides, nobody sees me in the Jacuzzi except you gals and I really don't care if you see my "extra bubbles." As if you don't make any bubbles yourself, Linda.")*

STELLA.   *(Looking at computer)* Oh my God!

LINDA.   What? Is it Microsoft? Are they being investigated for antitrust and RICO violations again? Did Bill Gates die? Don't tell me! What?

STELLA.   No. No news on Microsoft, just a fickle market, although Inteqcomp released poor earnings for the last quarter which temporarily halted its stock. This is much worse than that!

LINDA.   I have about two and a half million invested info-tech stocks thanks to your advice may I remind you? What could possibly be worse than that?

(ROSEMARY returns to her suite she shares with STELLA, eating BETH's breakfast.)

STELLA. Hush up and listen to this. *(SHE reads from computer screen)* "The *New York Times*, Monday, September 10. The Federal Department of Corrections announced today its tentative plans to close its Delaware Valley Federal Correctional facility. Delval is a low-level security prison that primarily houses criminals convicted of white collar crime. Inmates will be relocated to other prisons including Black Rock and Stone Ridge."

ROSEMARY. What?

LINDA. No!

STELLA. *(Continues to read the computer screen and "scrolls down" for the rest of the story)* "The Department of Corrections states that Delval's closing is due to insufficient resources and the recent reduction in Federal taxes enacted by the Republicans. Unless additional funding for the prison can be obtained, closing is scheduled by year end."

LINDA. There must be some mistake!

STELLA. *(Continues to read screen)* "Currently incarcerated at Delval are several notorious female felons including Dr. Linda Robertson, former CEO of the now defunct Fielweil HMO who is serving a 20 year sentence for Medicaid fraud, Stella Wild, former Wall Street Stock mogul sentenced to 15 years for insider trading which resulted in Black Friday in 1999, Beth Ziegler, computer genius, sentenced to 5 years for computer hacking, mail fraud and negotiating bogus real estate and commodities transactions via the Internet. Ziegler is scheduled to be released on parole today."

ROSEMARY. I don't believe this!

STELLA. Closing the prison at the end of the year? Beth left just in time. Damn Republicans and their tax cuts. I always vote Democrat just for that reason. Wait until my Congresswoman hears from me!

7

LINDA. *(Goes to computer and reads from screen)* "Inmates will be relocated to Black Rock and Stone Ridge"? Over my dead body! I'll take a lethal injection before I'd even consider relocating to either of those dumps.

ROSEMARY. Hey, my name isn't mentioned. I'm just as accomplished a felon as you are. In fact, my deeds are dirtier than yours and Beth's put together. How could they fail to mention that glorious day in 1997 when seven of the world's major global financial institutions closed their platinum gilded doors forever? I was behind that, you know. Not even a mention. I feel quite slighted.

LINDA. How can you joke about a thing like this? We are in serious jeopardy of losing the good thing we've got going here.

STELLA. Where the hell is Lucille? I'm going to page her. Why didn't she tell us about this? I'll bet that she has no idea.

(Picks up cell phone and dials page for **LUCILLE***)*

I'll be damned if I'm going to wind up in some dismal prison with common criminals. My God, they have murderers, robbers, psychos and who knows what else in those places!

LINDA. Okay, calm down. Obviously the Warden must know something about this. I'll shoot him an e-mail him that we need to convene an emergency meeting. *(SHE goes to her own laptop in her suite to order the food on-line. Alternatively, she can use a hand held device.)*

ROSEMARY. Not only that! The food! Can you just imagine. That reminds me. I'm hungry. Stella, e-mail our order to Buddha Bistro, okay? Anybody else in the mood for Chinese?

STELLA. Yeah, I am. What does everyone want? The usual?

LINDA. Whatever, fine. Just let me finish here first with my message to the Warden. Oh, don't forget to specify NO MSG! I couldn't wear my rings for a week the last time we ordered Chinese because Lucille forgot to tell them NO MSG! It's simply not an advisable food additive for women over 40.

STELLA. Yes, doctor.

(STELLA places the order on line.)

(LUCILLE enters rubbing her neck.)

LUCILLE. Whew! I'm exhausted. Beth wouldn't stop hugging me goodbye at the car. God, for a little thing she's pretty strong. My damn neck hurts. I got your page, Stella. You ordering lunch? I'm in the mood for Italian.

ROSEMARY. Sorry, it's Chinese today. Were ordered our usual, hope you don't mind.

LUCILLE. No, come to think of it, I have a taste for an egg roll and some shrimp fried rice. Did you order a PuPu platter for sharing, too?

STELLA. Lucille, did you read the paper today?

LUCILLE. Girl, now when did I have a chance to read the paper? You know all morning I was running around making sure Beth was packed, and getting her paperwork in order, and getting her trunks and boxes ready for overnight pickup in addition to taking care of you divas who are not leaving. By the way, Rosemary, your dry cleaning will be back on Friday.

LINDA. *(Returning to STELLA and ROSEMARY's suite.)* Well, well, Cinderella, just remember who your fairy godmothers are.

LUCILLE. Hey, I'm not complaining, believe me. But, on top of all that I'm supposed to be working on my thesis and I hardly have had a chance to start my research because I'm too busy wiping your pampered posteriors.

ROSEMARY. You better finish that thesis! We have a lot invested in you. Don't you dare disappoint us.

LUCILLE. Now, you know I'd never do that, Rosemary. If it wasn't for you girls I would have never earned my Bachelor's Degree let alone be finishing up my Master's. I know I owe you

9

all big-time. But come on, when the hell do I have time to look at a newspaper?

STELLA. I didn't think so. Come here. Read this.

(LUCILLE reads screen)

LUCILLE. What the hell? Is this some kind of a joke?

LINDA. We didn't think you knew.

LUCILLE. I had no clue about this! This must be a mistake. Otherwise, I'll be out of a job. Working for you girls is the best job I've ever had.

LINDA. Technically, Ceil, your employer is the Department of Corrections. We are just a secondary source of tax-free income and undiscloseable perks.

LUCILLE. Well, is this a nightmare or what? What are we going to do about it? Anyway, I thought you and the Warden had all of the finances for this place straightened out and the red ink turned back to black.

(ROSEMARY returns to her suite to place the yogurt back on the tray. Then SHE goes to Linda's laptop.)

STELLA. We did—that is—we do. . . The ink is black or it damn well better be. Damn that Warden. This prison is no more in financial hardship than we are, including you, Lucille. We made sure of that. Wait until I get my hands on that S.O.B.

LINDA. Wait a minute, Stella. Do you think he's been skimming from the financial holes we've been plugging?

STELLA. I don't know, but one thing is for sure: I'm going to find out.

ROSEMARY. *(Looking at computer screen)* Look, here's Warden's auto-reply. *(SHE reads screen)* Damn. "Warden Bird is out of the office and will reply to your message when he returns." How convenient. I'm sure he planned to be away just when the news broke. The coward. I never completely trusted him.

LINDA. You never completely trust any man.

ROSEMARY. Do you blame me? Look where it got you! Your lover–slash–business–partner testified against you in return for his own immunity. What a guy!

STELLA. Ladies, not that tired old tune again. Please.

ROSEMARY. *(ROSEMARY returns to her own suite.)* Lucille, did you know that Warden was going to be away? Where is he and when is he coming back?

LINDA. How can we reach him? Is he at home?

LUCILLE. I have no idea where the man is. He doesn't ask my permission to take time off. That works the "other" way. And, for the record, I never trusted him either.

STELLA. None of us "trust" Warden. It's just that we need the dirty bum as much as he needs us. The problem is he probably figured that out by now—dumb as he is—and the schmuck thinks he can have the upper hand sometimes. Ladies, we really need to do a better job of showing him who the boss is around here. He was nothing until we arrived on the scene. No one respected him, the place was a shambles, and he was burned out, bummed out, and on his way out because he couldn't turn the place around.

LUCILLE. Well, I know this isn't the best time to tell you, but I have more news.

LINDA. Good or bad? Send us an e-mail. We'll open it tomorrow. I think it's safe to assume that we've reached our bad news quota for the day.

LUCILLE. Well, it's not great news, but it's not terrible, either.

STELLA. Go ahead, Ceil, make our day.

LUCILLE. *(To LINDA)* You're getting a new cellmate.

ROSEMARY. We prefer to use the term either "suite-mate" or "contemporaneous cohabitant". Cellmate sounds so bourgeois.

LINDA. That's it? No problem. I was anticipating that. I don't mind company.

ROSEMARY. Hold on. There's more to it, isn't there? All right, give it up Lucille. Who is she?

STELLA. *(Gasps)* Don't tell me—they finally nailed the President's wife for tax evasion!

ROSEMARY. Of course! The First Lady! I knew they'd get her sooner or later. This is so exciting!

LINDA. Yeah—well, she still gets the top bunk. I've got clout around here.

ROSEMARY. I heard she has the same cosmetic surgeon as Michael Jackson. I wonder if we could arrange some outpatient sessions. I've been thinking about lip enhancements and liposuction.

LUCILLE. Calm down. It's not the First Lady.

ROSEMARY. Damn.

LINDA. Then who is it? Do we know her?

LUCILLE. I doubt it. Name is Sharon Watson. Twenty-eight. Divorced. One daughter. First-timer. Woman's a wreck. She arrived last Friday but has been in the infirmary on suicide watch ever since. She'll be joining you tomorrow morning unless she finds some way to harm herself tonight. I met her yesterday, and, other than being a basket case she seems very pleasant—cooperative. Insists she's innocent.

LINDA. Of course, we're all innocent!

STELLA. If you won't take our word—just ask Ken Lay and his innocent Enron buddies. They'll vouch for us, right gals?

LUCILLE. Would you be serious?

STELLA. I am serious, dear.

LINDA. Get back to...what's her name?

LUCILLE. Sharon Watson.

LINDA. Doesn't ring a bell.

STELLA. I've never heard of her.

ROSEMARY. Neither have I.

LINDA. What's she in for? Extortion?

LUCILLE. No.

LINDA. Bribery?

LUCILLE. Nuh-uh.

LINDA. Blackmail?

LUCILLE. Nope.

LINDA. Insurance fraud?

LUCILLE. Wrong.

LINDA. Money-laundering?

LUCILLE. No.

LINDA. Antitrust violations?

LUCILLE. Guess again.

STELLA. We are not in the mood for guessing games right now, Lucille. What?

LUCILLE. Murder One.

LINDA. Murder One! *(To* **LUCILLE***)* Absolutely, positively, definitely NOT! I refuse to share my life, my suite, my intimate thoughts, professional medical expertise or my sushi with a murderer. You know that. Are you crazy? She's liable to knife me in my sleep if we mess up her take-out order. Put her somewhere else.

STELLA. Lucille. We agreed—if you remember, with Warden's consent—to keep this little club of ours exclusive. I hate to sound prejudiced. However, we will only accept members with backgrounds similar to our own. That is, only money launderers, computer hackers, embezzlers, counterfeiters and similar non-violent "genteel" criminals are acceptable to us. We have our professionalism and dignity to maintain. We will not tolerate sharing our suites, meals or professional advice with murders, rapists, child molesters, pornographers or violent

13

criminals of any nature. You'll simply have to find other accommodations for Ms. Watson.

LUCILLE. I told you it wasn't good news but there's really nothing I can do about this until Warden gets back. Sorry girls. Anyway, she hasn't been convicted yet. Her trial isn't until December. Remember, our constitution says that she is innocent until proven guilty.

LINDA. Then why the hell is she in here instead of out on bail or over at Black Rock? That's where they keep dangerous criminals awaiting trial. If she doesn't have a prior offense how come she's not out on bail?

ROSEMARY. Wait until I get my hands on Warden and give him a piece of my mind. If he thinks we're sending him and Mrs. Bird on another Christmas cruise this year he is sadly mistaken!

LUCILLE. Now, just calm down a minute. I met Sharon when I had to arrange for her transport to the infirmary before I realized she'd be taking Beth's place. Poor kid. She's scared to death. She couldn't make bail because she doesn't own a home and had no one to make bond for her. She has no record and never had so much as a traffic violation—until now. She misses her kid and she's a mental wreck. Don't pass judgment. Come to think of it, she reminds me of Beth when she first came here a couple of years ago. She even looks like she could be related—a cousin or younger sister.

STELLA. Whose life has she extinguished?

LUCILLE. "Allegedly" extinguished. Ex-husband's new wife.

LINDA. How?

LUCILLE. Poison in her coffee. When she and the "ex" came to pick up the kid for the weekend. Kid wasn't there yet so she gave them coffee while they waited.

LINDA. Poison! Then it's worse than I thought! What if she tries to taint my food? How will I ever be sure of what I'm eating or drinking with her in my suite?

14

STELLA. Well, Doc, it may be good for you to drop a few pounds.

LINDA. If you think it's so funny, she can move in with you. We'll switch suites right now. I'm sure Lucille doesn't care, right Lucille?

LUCILLE. No, that's fine with me. What's another seven tons of paperwork among friends? Stella, okay with you? I'll start blazing the paper trail.

ROSEMARY. Just one second. I'm affected by this decision too, you know. Linda, I love you like a sister, but you snore like a horny bullfrog. If Stella suites with the murderer that means that you suite with me. You'll have do something about your snoring or write me a prescription for sleeping pills because I'll strangle you in your sleep if she doesn't poison you first.

LINDA. I don't snore, you're making that up.

STELLA. I hate to break it to you, Linda, but Rosemary is right—you do sound like a broken buzz saw when you get going some nights.

LINDA. Too bad, Rosemary is stuck with me. I can't help if it you're a light sleeper. Besides, Beth never complained. I think that a mild sleep aid at bedtime would probably do you good, Rose.

STELLA. Listen, our goal is to get rid of her completely, not shuffle her from your suite to mine. Linda, the murderer bunks with you until we can arrange to have her moved elsewhere. Lucille, I'd rather you start on the paperwork for her transfer to a different section—far away from us—and you can start by figuring out what space is available and who can be rearranged, if necessary. That way all Warden will have to do when he returns is sign off on it because you will have taken care of the details.

ROSEMARY. *(To* **STELLA***)* Well, things can't get much worse than this, now can it? Beth is basking on the beach by now and hating every minute of it. Our elegant existence is in danger of extinction. And, for the icing on the proverbial cake, we've got a murderess as a houseguest.

STELLA. Always the optimist, aren't you Rosemary!

ROSEMARY.   Well, what is there to be optimistic about? Our haven is going to hell in a handcart.

STELLA.   That is precisely the inherent difference in us, I guess. I see the opportunity in situations like this and you see the threats.

LUCILLE.   Obviously that's because of your varied professional backgrounds. Of course Rosemary sees the threats, she's an attorney. She's trained to look for the pitfalls and play devil's advocate in every situation. You, on the other hand, Stella, are an investment analyst and broker. You are an expert at turning garbage into gold. Linda, you are the most likely one to keep a clear perspective about this situation. Try to think of this upheaval as a seriously ill patient.   With your medical expertise, what course of treatment would you recommend?

LINDA. Assisted suicide.

(BLACKOUT)

Act 1~Scene 2

(TIME: One week later.)

(AT RISE: **SHARON**, *the "new kid on the Block" is sobbing quietly to herself in her "suite". SHE hears* **LUCILLE** *coming from stage right, stops crying and pretends to be asleep.* **LUCILLE** *wears a headphones and SHE is singing and "dancing" to a song on a portable radio clipped to her belt.* **LUCILLE** *carries with her four roses and a fancy box of chocolates.* **LUCILLE** *proceeds to tidy up Stella and Rosemary's suite as SHE sings and dances. SHE places a rose and piece of chocolate on their beds. SHE also helps herself to a splash of Rosemary's perfume and helps herself to a piece (or two) of the chocolate.* *[SHE may even try on an article of clothing or hat while in Stella and Rosemary's suite because SHE feels totally "at home" and would not be troubled if they came in and found her among their possessions.]* **LUCILLE** *finishes up in Stella and Rosemary's suite then proceeds to Linda and Sharon's suite still singing and dancing.* **LUCILLE**, *who then sees* **SHARON** *sleeping, stops singing but continues to mouth words and continues to dance "quietly" so as not to wake* **SHARON**. **LUCILLE** *finishes a quick tidy-up of that room and puts a rose and candy on Linda's bed. SHE then puts a rose and flower on the nightstand next to Sharon's bed and takes a cover/comforter from the bottom of the bed and puts it over her. SHE exits Stage Left dancing/humming softly to herself. After* **LUCILLE** *exits,* **SHARON** *sits up and looks around at the tidied room and looks quizzically at the candy/flower on her nightstand.*

17

SHE begins to cry softly once again at the circumstance of her incarceration. **LINDA**, **ROSEMARY** *and* **STELLA**. *return from their workout at the Delval Fitness Center. They are wearing fashionable workout clothes/gym shoes with towels around their necks.)*

ROSEMARY. God, what a workout. I'm exhausted.

STELLA.   So, what do you think of my new personal trainer?

ROSEMARY. He looks gay.

LINDA.   So what. She didn't hire him for that kind of a workout... *(Beat)* did you?

STELLA.   Oh, come on now. You know me better than that. He's way to young for me. I like my men very old and very rich.

*(THEY laugh as they enter Rosemary/Stella's "room". **LINDA** notices **SHARON** is on her bed, crying.)*

LINDA.   I can't stand this one more minute. She's been doing this all week. My nerves are shot. If she doesn't knock off the boo-hooing or get the hell out of here I'm calling her judge myself to have her transferred—or executed. I went to Penn with her judge, you know. I'm sure I can think of a favor or two Big Jim still owes me.

STELLA.   Big Jim?

LINDA.   *(Gives a sly smirk)*   Very Big Jim. Let's not go there, shall we?

ROSEMARY. Has she said anything to you yet? She hasn't said a word to me. I think she's afraid of us.

STELLA.   Afraid of us? That's insane. We're the ones who ought to be frightened of her. She's the murderess, not us. *(To*

18

LINDA) Do you still have Lucille taste your food before you eat it?

LINDA. Yes, but I'm running out of excuses. I have to tell her that I think it may be too spicy or that I'm not hungry and she needs to share what I'm having. Lucille is bound to get suspicious as to why I'm sharing my meals with her. Last evening she consumed half of my Crab Imperial and it was a small portion to begin with. Remind me to speak with the chef at Le Trout about not being so skimpy.

ROSEMARY. I'm stiffening up. What time is Fredrico coming to give us our massages?

STELLA. Nails today, Rosemary. Massages tomorrow. You're a day off schedule. Kim Li and her staff will be here at 4:00 for our manicures and pedicures. I'm thinking about another waxing too though it's only been 5 days. *(SHE picks up mirror from dresser to examine her face/neck.)* With each passing year I seem to get more and more hair in stranger and stranger places. *(SHE peeks inside of her blouse.)*

LINDA. Three words. Hormone Replacement Therapy. I keep telling you that but will you listen? I can arrange to have a prescription delivered for you. It's really not as controversial as they make it out to be. You do realize that menopause is just around the corner.

STELLA. Thank you so much for reminding me, doctor.

LINDA. Misery loves company.

ROSEMARY. Perhaps Lucille can give me a back rub. I think I strained too hard in aerobics class.

(SHARON loudly blows her nose.)

LINDA. That's it. I'm going to give her a piece of my mind. She's got some nerve coming in here and thinking she can turn our fiesta into a funeral home.

STELLA. Hold on, you'll really scare her. Let me try to talk to her.

19

(STELLA goes next door to Linda/Sharon's cell.
ROSEMARY *and* **LINDA** *listen right outside)*

Hi Sharon. How are you today dear?

(No response from **SHARON***)*

Now listen. We know you're upset, but you've been here a week
now, right?

*(***SHARON** *nods her head)*

It's not so bad, now is it? In fact, if you make the best of it, it's
kind of fun.

(No response from **SHARON***)*

Sharon, honey, you've got to pull yourself together. Just because
you murdered your ex-husband's wife in a jealous rage doesn't
mean...

SHARON. I DIDN'T DO IT!

ROSEMARY. *(Enters, reassuringly)* Of course you didn't!
What Stella meant to say is that just because you got arrested for
killing some slut who stole your...

SHARON. She wasn't a slut! I didn't do it. She is—was—a
nice woman. I didn't kill her. Why won't anyone believe me?

STELLA. We do believe you. Why don't you tell us about
it? We're good listeners, and we're certainly not going anywhere.
Anyway, it's not so bad here with us, is it?

SHARON. I feel like I'm stuck in the middle of a bizarre
nightmare. Where am I? In prison or at a European Spa? Who
are you women? This is jail, isn't it? It's not at all what I

20

imagined. I keep expecting someone to pop in with a video camera and say, "Smile, Sharon. You're on *Candid Camera*."

LINDA. *(Entering the room)* You ungrateful little snob! All week I've been killing myself—pardon the pun—going out of my way to be nice to you. We're regular people making the best out of bad circumstances. Fortunately, we happen to have the resources and connections to do it. All week now I've tried to include you in our activities. You could have come to aerobics with us, but NO, you wanted to stay here sniffling and crying in the cell—which, by the way, we refer to as our "suite". Well, that's just fine with me. From now on you can eat poison—er—prison food. No more gourmet deliveries for you! You waste everything we order for you anyway. You must have lost five pounds since you arrived.

SHARON. Nine. I lost nine.

ROSEMARY. Well, honey, that's not good! You've got to keep up your strength. You've got your trial in December. How about we get some prime rib tonight. From Harry's on Eighth? Melt in your mouth. You like prime rib?

SHARON. *(Nods)* How do you do all this? I never dreamed that you have your meals catered in prison. And, you have a masseur three times each week? That's outrageous.

LINDA. Don't knock it until you've tried it, darling.

SHARON. That's not what I mean. It's just...this is so...different...from what I expected...and... What's with the guard, Lucille? She seems...so...

STELLA. Friendly?

SHARON. Exactly. I thought prison guards were supposed to be mean and bossy, and she's... *(SHE starts tearing up again)* I'm just having a hard time trying to sort all this out. I feel like I'm in the *Twilight Zone* or something. *(Blows her nose loudly)*

ROSEMARY. Sweetheart, with the way you're going through tissues I'm going to have to ask Stella to include paper stocks in my investment portfolio—or better yet—forestry futures. Sharon, we are here because we deserve to be. We've "gone against the system" and it caught up with us.

SHARON. I don't understand.

LINDA. Let me introduce you to your new friends. Sharon Watson, meet Rosemary Adams. Rosemary is here because she used her J.D. in Law and MBA in Finance to inure funds to her own benefit instead of to the good of the bank that employed her as Senior Vice President and General Counsel. *(Wagging her finger at Rosemary)* Shame on you, Rosemary! Now, turning to Stella Wild, let us assure you Michael Milken could learn some lessons from our gal Stella! Wall Street has yet to recover and perhaps never will from the likes of our own "Wall Street Wizard", as they referred to our gal Stella in her heyday—that is, before the market crashed with Stella holding the cash.

STELLA. Linda, I'm blushing. You give me too much credit.

LINDA. And, now for *moi*. I am—that is, I was, prior to my conviction and the revocation of my license—a skilled doctor of medicine. My specialty was cardiology. In fact, I am responsible for the first transplant of a morbidly obese patient's human heart with that of a walrus. It's been over twenty years now and I'm proud to say that my patient is still thriving.

STELLA. Yes, Linda receives a holiday photo every year from his caretaker at the Baltimore Aquarium.

LINDA. *(Ignoring STELLA.)* Ultimately, I traded in my stethoscope and scalpel for the guts and glory of running a managed care organization. The prognosis of my HMO was healthy and hearty until, of course, the Office of the Investigator General decided to pursue fraud and abuse allegations against several of our affiliated physicians' practices. To make a long and dull story short, in the end I was found to be guilty of defrauding Medicare and Medicaid for personal gain. Ha! Of course, the conspirators who testified against me avoided jail sentences for cooperating with the Feds. While here I sit for ten-or-so more years, pretending to appeal and kick and scream about injustice of it all when really, I'm just damn glad to finally be out of the rat race.

SHARON. Your stories are amazing. I would have never imagined that professional women like you could wind up in jail. Are you married? How do your husbands and families cope with you in prison?

> *(During Stella's next "speech",* **LINDA** *falls asleep and starts to snore—loudly at times.* **ROSEMARY** *retrieves a box of crackers and tin of caviar and begins to eat, tuning* **STELLA** *out.* **STELLA** *delivers the following monologue while swinging her tennis racket and/or holding two tennis balls. The only one interested in what she has to say is Sharon—who is very attentive.)*

STELLA. I think I can speak to that on behalf of all of us. Prior to our convictions—totally unrelated—I should point out. That is, we didn't know each other or become acquainted until after we arrived at Delval . We worked around the clock at our respective occupations. Having been the product of Ivy League Universities, we are well educated and were driven to break the proverbial "glass ceilings" that precluded women for years from reaching the top of the corporate ladder. Oh, we were highly motivated by the money, the power, the desire to be "the woman who made it to the top"—ahead of our male colleagues and counterparts in the corporate world. *(STELLA holds two tennis balls in one hand and unwittingly makes a Freudian quasi-obscene gesture with the balls. SHE realizes what she has done, clears her throat and regains composure.)* We enjoyed the professional notoriety—being a "Who's Who"—having our names on the "A" lists. We allowed our careers to consume us. We had no time—or desire—to form friendships let alone have meaningful romantic relationships or families. Vacations? Ha! An utter waste of time. We traveled so much we never knew from day-to-day in

23

what city, state, or hotel room we would wake up in. In the end, the temptations inherent in our professions led to our ultimate demise and …the rest is history. Now we enjoy—no—we savor our solitude and relish our friendships with each other. We have become for each other the family and friends we sacrificed when the rat race consumed us.

ROSEMARY. Well said, Stella. I agree completely.

LINDA. *(Loudly snorting herself awake)* So do I. My sentiments exactly.

SHARON. That's incredible. You really like it here then?

STELLA. Delval reminds me of my college days. Being here is like the best part of being in my old college dorm. I can party all night with my best buddies without worrying about having to drag myself out of bed for an early class or cramming all night for an exam.

SHARON. You mean, you are actually happy?

LINDA. Happy? Hmmm. Are you happy Stella?

STELLA. Define "happy".

ROSEMARY. We are not unhappy, Sharon. Of course, we don't *like* being in prison or the stigma attached to being in jail. Without a doubt we have ruined our professional lives. But, we have accepted it, and as they say, we have turned our lemons into margaritas!

STELLA. That's not exactly how the saying goes, Rosie.

ROSEMARY. I know but it is almost cocktail hour and I could use a drink right now. Besides, I got her to smile for the first time in a week. *(To* **SHARON.***)* Admit it, you just grinned and it didn't kill you, did it?

*(***SHARON*** shakes her head and gives a meek grin)*

STELLA. When we do leave Delval we will move on, hopefully to better things. For now—since we did the crime, we do the time. Lucky for us, we have the means to have some control over how we spend our time at Delval to make our lives bearable. Also, we have the time to reflect on our past. Sure, sometimes we get depressed, but we can count on each other to snap us out of it, keep our spirits up, keep us looking forward not backward. Right, ladies?

ROSEMARY AND **LINDA**. Right/Sure.

ROSEMARY. If all we did was focus on where we screwed up we'd never be able to get out of bed in the morning. Instead, we focus on other things, like each other and completely trivial things like manicures and pedicures—things that we never took the time to enjoy before we came. We have made Delval the garden where we have stopped to smell the roses. Linda, give me an example of something that you would have never considered doing before but you now enjoy because of the extra time on your hands here at Delval.

LINDA. That's easy. Sleep late! Or, read a good mystery. Sharon, you are welcome to have a look at my book collection and borrow anything you like.

ROSEMARY. Stella?

STELLA. Definitely movies! I'm catching up on years of great films that I missed because I was always working. I have quite a DVD collection now. Before Delval I think the last film I saw must have been either *"Butch Cassidy and the Sundance Kid"* or *"The Graduate"*. Let me tell you, Robert Redford and Dustin Hoffman have certainly aged since then.

ROSEMARY. That's your opinion. They still look good to me.

STELLA. Sharon, I have a pretty nice DVD collection that you're welcome to any time, plus you may have noticed we have digital cable as well as "the dish".

ROSEMARY. As for me, I now enjoy being able to have time to indulge—or—as my friends here will tell you, on occasion, "overindulge" in good food and fine wine. After so many years of conference room fare and lukewarm industrial strength coffee gulped down over contract negotiations into the

25

wee hours of the night, it's simply wonderful to have time to enjoy a relaxing meal and fine bottle of wine.

LINDA. Don't forget exercise. Before Delval none of us had time to devote to fitness. Now, fitness and exercise are a part of our daily routine. *(LINDA attempts to bend over and touch her toes then decides that it is not worth the energy.)*

ROSEMARY. I must admit, I really didn't miss not exercising. My back still aches. I know I pulled a muscle this afternoon.

SHARON. I have another question if you don't mind. The Guard—it appears that she works for you. Does she?

STELLA. Just put it into perspective. Lucille is good to us because we're good to her. Besides that, she really is a nice person. We provided her with the resources, financial and otherwise, to attend evening college. She has a B.S. in criminal justice and is about to earn her Masters Degree. We help each other. Know what I mean?

SHARON. So you bribe her?

LINDA. Bribe is such an ugly word, dear. We don't *bribe* anyone. We simply convince them that it is better too be mutually advantaged rather than singularly disadvantaged.

STELLA. We're getting sidetracked here. Why don't you tell us about you? If you're innocent why are you here? Why do they think you killed—what's her name?

SHARON. Diane. Her name is—was—Diane. Ben, that's my ex-husband—Ben and Diane came over to my shop to pick up Kristen, my—our—daughter for the weekend. Kristen's school is around the corner from the shop. They forgot, or Kristen forgot to tell them—that she had band practice after school. She's just learning to play the clarinet. She's seven—almost eight years old. I'm going to miss her birthday…
(Starts to cry again)

ROSEMARY. There, there now. Here's another tissue. Then what happened?

SHARON. Well, I had a few customers at the time so I gave them some coffee and they just waited for her to get there. When Kristen arrived they all left. The next thing I know Kristen calls me in hysterics from the hospital. Diane got violently ill on their way home, and she just died. It was awful. Kristen said she died on the way to the hospital.

LINDA. So, why do they think you did it?

SHARON. Well, they did an autopsy and found poison in her blood.

LINDA. What kind?

SHARON. That's the strange part. Rat poison. Why on earth would I put rat poison in Diane's coffee?

LINDA. Hmmmm. Sounds suspicious. Why would you even have rat poison?

SHARON. I kept some at the shop because one night when I was locking up I saw a rat, or some ugly thing that looked like a rat, rummaging around the garbage cans in the back alley when I was putting out that day's trash.

STELLA. What is it that you do? You know all about us now but we don't know a thing about you other than the kid, the ex and the ex's dead wife. What do you do for a living?

SHARON. I'm a hairdresser. I have my own little shop. "Sharon's Shears." It's in East Falls, very close to the city. I have no idea what's going to happen to it now.

ROSEMARY. An entrepreneur! Excellent! And so timely as well. Edmund has been charging exorbitant prices to come in every week and, quite frankly, I don't think his services have been up to snuff recently. Do you, Stella?

LINDA. Quiet, Rosemary. Let her finish her story. Then what happened?

SHARON. It was horrible. The most horrible and humiliating experience of my entire life.

(Lights dim and spotlight on SHARON as she tells her story)

I opened the shop the following morning and was working on my first customer, Mrs. Perelstein, when all of a sudden four policemen, actually, one was a police woman—they came in and read me my rights and handcuffed me right in front of her. I said, "Why are you doing this? I didn't do anything! Plus, I was right in the middle giving Mrs. Perelstein a perm. The poor woman had curlers and perm solution in her hair and I couldn't do anything about it because they were dragging me out in handcuffs. She was screaming, *(Imitating Mrs. Perelstein's voice)* "My hair! My hair!" There's a deli next door, which is what I think attracts the rats, and Mr. Jacobson, the deli owner, saw the police cars out front and heard all of the commotion. He probably thought my shop was being robbed. He came running over to see what was going on. I think he wound up finishing Mrs. Perelstein's permanent because she was screaming at me, *(Again imitating)* "You can't leave yet, you have to finish my hair." Mrs. Perelstein will probably sue me for a bad perm on top of everything else. Then they charged me and took my picture and fingerprinted me at the police station and put me on a prison bus to this place. When I got here they drugged me up and kept me on a suicide watch or something at the prison infirmary. I'm not going to kill myself for heaven sake! What would happen to Kristen? *(SHE cries yet again)*

(Spotlight off. Lights as they were)

LINDA. And, you're telling us, you SWEAR, you didn't kill Diane?

SHARON. I SWEAR. I had no reason to. She was a nice person. I liked her.

STELLA. You said before that she was too good for—what's his name again?

SHARON. Ben.

STELLA. Ben. What did you mean by that?

SHARON. Ben's just a jerk. He's good looking, very charming. He has a really big…ego. Once you get to know him you realize that he's not what he appears to be on the outside. He's selfish, arrogant, controlling and condescending. Then, once you marry him he turns into a full-fledged egotistical and narcissistic jerk! When we were married he cheated on me left and right. I was his second wife. I'm sure he cheated on the first one too.

LINDA. With you he was cheating on his first wife?

SHARON. Oh, no! She died before I even met him.

STELLA. Then how do you know he cheated on her?

SHARON. A leopard doesn't change its spots, right?

ROSEMARY. Good point. How did his first wife die?

SHARON. Car accident. The breaks went on her car when she was driving to work one morning. I understand that she crashed head on into a donut shop.

STELLA. Hmmm.

LINDA. How long were you married?

SHARON. Just about five years. I divorced him when Kristen was two. Why?

STELLA. Did you ever have anything "weird" happen to you when you were married?

SHARON. How do you mean?

LINDA. Like—any unusual illnesses, freak accidents, unusual things happen?

SHARON. Well, shortly after we were married I had a bike accident, but that wasn't his fault.

STELLA. What happened?

(Lights dim. Spotlight once again on **SHARON** *as she tells her story.)*

29

SHARON.   We went for a ride on the bike path down by the river. He had a bike before we were married because he was into fitness and exercise. I didn't have one so I bought a used 10 speed at a yard sale. It looked like it was in pretty good condition—or so I thought anyway—and I only paid thirty-five dollars for it. Anyway, a couple days after I bought it we took a ride down by the river and one of the pedals flew off of the bike as I'm picking up speed to go up a hill. The bike went one way and I flew the other way into the street. I cracked my head wide open on the curb, broke my arm and fractured two ribs. If a car had been coming I'd probably be dead. It happened so fast. I quickly learned the value of a bike helmet. I'll never go without one again and I don't let Kristin ride without one either—no matter how much she complains. I was in the hospital for over a week.

STELLA/LINDA/ROSEMARY.   Hmmm.

ROSEMARY.   What does Ben do for a living?

SHARON.   He a facilities manager.   He supervises maintenance staff—painters, plumbers, electricians.

ROSEMARY.   Did anything else happen to you when you were married?

SHARON.   Well, there was the time that the hair dryer fell into the tub. But fortunately I had just gotten out.

LINDA.   Where was Ben then?

SHARON.   Oh, right there. He was drying his hair and he accidentally dropped it because his hands were slippery from the hair gel he uses. Hey, wait a minute—where are you going with all this?

STELLA.   Honey, did Ben get any insurance money when his first wife died?

SHARON.   Oh yes. In fact, he also got a settlement against the car manufacturer and the service station that inspected the car. He got a lifetime supply of donuts too.

LINDA. This is getting better and better. What about when you were married? Did you have life insurance policies for each other? Oh, sure. Doesn't everybody?

STELLA. And, would it be safe to guess that poor old Diane was also worth more to him dead than alive?

SHARON. You don't think...?

ROSEMARY. That's exactly what we think! Now, the real question is, how to do we prove it? Did Ben use the rest room while he was there?

LINDA. Did he have access to where you kept the rat poison?

SHARON. No. In fact, he just sat next there and watched TV the whole time until Kristen arrived.

LINDA. What about Diane?

SHARON. I think she may have read a magazine or a hair style book. I was busy. I really didn't pay much attention to them.

LUCILLE. *(Entering with a drinks cart (or tray) and proceeds as she speaks to serve everyone their afternoon cocktail, including ,of course, herself.)* Look at this. Congratulations. You finally got "Little Bo Weep" to stop crying and start talking. Little girl, I was afraid to come near you for fear I'd slip on the wet floor and break my ankle from all those tears you've been leaking.

STELLA. Yes, I think we've made some progress. But, Lucille, the girl has real troubles. We think she's telling the truth. She claims she's innocent and I think it's pretty safe to say that we to believe her.

LINDA. Lucille, if this kid isn't innocent she sure as hell is a damn good liar.

LUCILLE. Ladies, she isn't the only one with real troubles. I don't know how to tell you this.

STELLA. What now?

LUCILLE. The word on the street is that this facility is not closing at the end of the year.

STELLA. That's a relief!

LUCILLE.   Wrong!   There was a memo from the Department of Corrections in my in-bin.   You are to be relocated to Black Rock or Stone Ridge with the next ten days. Most likely, you'll be split up. My job has been eliminated due to redundancy effective with Delval's closure. I'm sorry to tell you, the party's over.

> (THEY *all look at each other in total dismay then take a drink as the curtain closes.*)

CURTAIN

END OF ACT 1

Act II~Scene 1

*(AT RISE: **SHARON** is alone in her "suite." SHE is napping, having fallen asleep looking at a photo album of her daughter. **STELLA** is in her shared "suite" and is working on the laptop computer. **ROSEMARY, LINDA** and **LUCILLE** are offstage in the Warden's office having their nails done.)*

STELLA. *(Muttering to herself/computer)* Come on. That's the right password—I know it is. *(SHE bangs the keyboard in frustration)* Damn, why can't I get in?

(Stella's cell phone rings)

Hello. Oh, Beth! Good! You? I miss you too. Are your adjusting? Hang in there, it'll get easier. Oh, you heard, huh? Yes, you lucky thing—Delval is really closing and we're being split up at either Black Rock or Stone Ridge. I know, it's terrible! We've been up for two days straight trying to figure out what we can do about this. No, Warden Bird is conveniently out of his office. Nobody knows where he is, not even his wife—we called her. He told her he was going to a Federal Corrections Conference and he hasn't called home. He hasn't checked in with anyone here since he left. I'm trying to access his files right now because I have a feeling that the books are going to tell all. I know, I wish there is something you could do, too. No, they're not here. They're in the Warden's office with Lucille having their nails done. Okay, I'll have them give you a ring when they get back. Me too sweetie. Bye now.

33

(Enter **ROSEMARY** *and* **LINDA**. *Linda's cell phone rings in Sharon's cell—it wakes her up. SHE decides it would be okay to answer it when it does not stop ringing.)*

ROSEMARY. *(To* **STELLA***)* Any luck?

STELLA. None. I can't get into the prison's books and I'm really mad. He must have changed and secured a new password that I can't seem to crack. Looks like Warden Bird flew the proverbial coop. Even Mrs. Bird doesn't know where he is. The only difference is—she doesn't seem to care and we do.

(THEY all gather around **Stella**'s *laptop and watch as* **STELLA** *tries to break the code/password, quietly offering her "creative password suggestions" as the phone rings in Sharon's suite and* **SHARON** *answers it.)*

SHARON. *(Answering Linda's cell phone)* Hello. No, this is the right number. Oh, I see. I'm her new roommate. I think she'll be coming back soon. What? No, no, I understand. No, I won't. Okay. *(SHE hangs up)*

ROSEMARY. Sorry, did we wake you Sharon? We'll be quiet, go back to sleep. You need it—Linda said that you tossed and turned all night long.

SHARON. *(***SHARON** *joins the other's in Stella's suite)* I'm fine Rosemary. Your nails look nice.

LINDA. *(Entering Stella and Rosemary's suite)* I've been thinking. I may be onto something. Hear me out.

STELLA. Anything is worth a shot. What have you got?

LINDA. Beth is an expert at hacking. That's what landed her in here to begin with. She traded commodities that never existed and hacked into securities networks to make it look as though they did. I'm thinking if we ask her she can help us get into the prison's books or even get into them herself remotely from her laptop at the beach.

STELLA. Funny you should say that. She just called a minute ago because she heard the news all the way down in Palm Beach. She offered to help but I'm not sure we ought to get her involved in this. She's just getting her life back on track. I told her you'd call her.

ROSEMARY. I agree with Stella. Beth is younger than we are. She has a real shot to rebuild her career. I know she hated to leave us, but we all know deep down that it's better on the outside. Who knew that she'd be leaving in the nick of time? Once she adjusts to being on the outside she'll be fine.

SHARON. Oh, dear.

ROSEMARY. What, honey?

SHARON. Oh, nothing. I just...it's nothing.

LINDA. It's not nothing. What were you going to say? Say it.

SHARON. I promised I wouldn't say anything but now I'm not so sure. *(Pause)* Beth called just before you got back.

STELLA. How do you know? You were asleep.

SHARON. Well, I guess she called me right after she called you.

STELLA. Why would she call you? She doesn't even know you.

SHARON. I mean, you told her that Linda and Rosemary were having their nails done so she called Linda to leave a voice-mail message but I picked up the phone instead. She told me something that I promised her I wouldn't tell you.

STELLA. Why would she tell you anything she doesn't want us to know?

SHARON. It's not that. I guess she figured you'd be upset with her. She's worried about all of you and she said...she said...she told me that she's going to fly up here right away.

She'll be here tonight. She's sure she can help. I promised her I wouldn't tell you she was coming back.

ROSEMARY. Sharon, don't worry. It was right to tell us. We won't let her screw up her life again. It's not worth it.

LUCILLE. *(Entering breathlessly with letter)* You will never guess what I just found in Warden's office!

EVERYONE. What?

LUCILLE. Look at this.

ROSEMARY. It's a letter from the Department of Corrections.

LINDA. Let me see that. *(SHE takes letter and reads)* It's dated six months ago. He knew. All this time he knew plans were underway to close Delval and he never told us. Listen to this.... *(SHE reads)* "Dear Warden Bird" blah blah blah "...despite your significant managerial and enforcement contributions to cut costs and achieve savings and redundancy targets at the Delaware Valley Correctional facility, it is the recommendation and decision of the Department that economies of scale can be better achieved by combining the resources and populations of the Delaware Valley facility with those of other facilities. Accordingly, we intend to announce the closure of the Delaware Valley Correctional Facility by or before the close of the fourth quarter of this year." That son-of-a-bitch. It makes perfect sense now as to why it didn't matter where Sharon was incarcerated and that she was put in with us. Everyone will wind up getting shuffled around anyway at the other prisons.

STELLA. We taught Warden too well, girls. Lucille, you are going to have to inform the Department that Warden is AWOL. The trouble is, they won't care unless we can prove that he skimmed the funds we've been providing to keep this place operational and efficient. We can't do that without getting ourselves into more trouble for unlawful access and manipulation of Federal information technology and data. He's got us over a barrel and he knows it.

SHARON. I don't understand why they wouldn't care that he's missing.

ROSEMARY. Because on the surface it doesn't appear that he misappropriated anything unless we can access the books to determine that funds were, in fact, misappropriated. Besides, you know the government, they'll just be glad that he's not around to collect his pension.

SHARON. Won't they suspect foul play?

STELLA. It's hard to prove foul play if nothing is amiss. They'll probably think that he simply got another job in light of the prison closing and didn't bother to tell anybody. We've got to prove otherwise.

LINDA. Where would he have gone? Lucille, any ideas?

LUCILLE. No, but don't forget my criminal justice background. Half of my classmates are either cops or private investigators. I may be able get someone to help us.

ROSEMARY. Do you know anyone well enough to help us discreetly? Of course, we would reward them for their discretion. But they'd have to act fast and they'd have to be trustworthy.

LUCILLE. In fact, I do. One of my classmates, Tamara Johnson, runs her own investigative agency. I'll call her right away. Her number is in the address book in my locker. I was going to give her a call anyway since I've been thrown to the sharks in the job market. Maybe she can give me some employment leads.

LINDA. Lucille, I have no doubt that when this all shakes out, you'll land on your feet. You are smart, intelligent, and hardworking. I'll be glad to make some calls for you and give you the name of some of my contacts. You'll have no trouble finding a new and better job. Oh, when Beth gets here I want her to hook up with your friend. I hate to say this but Beth is probably going to have to do some outside hacking. Will your friend cooperate?

LUCILLE. Thanks for the vote of confidence. I'm not so sure I agree with you about the "better job" part though. I'm going to miss you girls, that's for sure. I really hope that Tamara will cooperate with us—it's worth a try—especially if the price is right.

STELLA. Its' right.

LUCILLE. Got it. *(Exits)*

(BLACKOUT)

Act II~Scene 2

(SETTING: Same—Later that evening.)

(AT RISE: Cells are empty. BETH arrives in a flashy trench coat, scarf and large sunglasses (very Jackie Kennedy Onassis chic) and looks around in a "familiar" sort of homesick way. SHE sits on her old bunk/bed (now Sharon's bed) and removes her shoes. She is just about to lie down when SHARON enters.)

SHARON. (Entering and seeing BETH about to lie down in her bed, politely) Oh, excuse me.

BETH. (Rising) Oh, I'm so sorry. Sharon?

SHARON. Beth?

BETH. Sorry about your bed. It used to be mine.

SHARON. I wish it still were, if you know what I mean. No offense.

BETH. None taken. Stella sent me an e-mail about your situation. I'm sorry.

SHARON. So am I, thanks.

BETH. Where is everyone? They're usually here at this hour watching a DVD or "Magnum PI" reruns.

SHARON. After dinner, Lucille snuck them into the Warden's office. They didn't want me to go with them in case they got caught by one of the new guards. They say I've got enough of my own troubles without getting into any more.

BETH. How are you coping? I remember when I first arrived at Delval I was completely devastated. I thought my life was over. Then, I met Rosemary and Stella and Linda, and when it was time for me to leave I didn't want to go!

SHARON. I know, they told me all about you.

BETH.   Are you taking care of yourself?   You've got to remember to eat or you'll get sick. Are you sleeping okay?

SHARON.   Well, your friends are plotting to fatten me up, that's for sure.   I never had gourmet food until I arrived in prison.   But, I'm really not sleeping very well.   As soon as I put my head down, a million thoughts seem to run through my head all at once and I can't get to sleep. Plus, Linda snores.

BETH.   You're telling me!   You'll get use to it.   After a while she begins to sound like a freight going down the tracks, whoo-whooo-whoo-whooo; once you get into her rhythm it actually becomes therapeutic.   Now I can't sleep unless I'm on a train to DC or New York.   *(Looking at Sharon's pictures)*   Is that your daughter?   She's pretty. She looks like you.   *(THEY look in the mirror together)*   Stella mentioned that she thinks you look like me when I first got here.   Of course, I was younger then...but we do have a resemblance—she was right.

SHARON.   Stella told me that I remind her of you.   It's a real coincidence isn't it?   Then again, my whole prison experience thus far has been one weird occurrence after another.   *(SHE gets the framed picture of her daughter)*.   This is Kristen.   Tomorrow is her 8th birthday.   I miss her so much.   People say she's starting to look more like me.   When she was little she was the image of her father.   *(SHE finds a picture of the three of them in her photo album)*   See.   She was only two here.   This was taken when we went to...   *(HER voice cracks—SHE can't continue)*

BETH.   *(Looking at the picture)*   Hey, I know him. Benny. . . *(SHE recalls)*   ...Benny Watson, right? He's your husband?

SHARON.   Ex-husband. You know Ben?

BETH.   We went to high school together—I haven't seen him in 15 years I guess.   I thought I heard through the alumni grapevine that his wife died.

SHARON.   She did.   I'm his second wife. His third wife is dead too—I'm the only one that survived marriage to him.   That's why I'm here.   I guess Stella also told you about that in her e-mails. They think that I poisoned his third wife. He made me out to be the jealous ex-wife.

BETH. Stella mentioned that. Too bad. I'm sorry. I probably shouldn't say this but he was a real jerk in school—but...that was a long time ago. People change. He's still good looking though, very fit. I think he ran track.

SHARON. Yeah, he works out all the time. He's a real fitness freak and totally vain about his appearance. And you're right about the jerk part...don't apologize.

BETH. Small world. Bennie Watson.

SHARON. Your friends think that he had something to do with Diane's death. She was his third wife. They think he somehow poisoned her and made it look like I did it out of scorn and jealousy. I didn't scorn the woman—I pitied her for getting involved with him.

BETH. Now that I think of it, I'm almost positive he was kicked out in our senior year. He didn't graduate with the class. Some scandal about stealing money or something from the teacher's lounge and he tried to pin it on one of the janitors. I think they found a wallet or something that belonged to one of the teachers in his gym locker. It's so long ago now I forget. Bennie was bad news—always scamming somebody for something. Cute though—a real charmer until you got to know him. Isn't it ironic? I was class Valedictorian, and he was expelled for stealing. Which of us would you have wagered would have wound up in prison?

SHARON. He hasn't changed much, believe me—he's still up to no good.

BETH. I used to feel kind-of sorry for him. He was bounced around from one foster home to another. For a while I think he even lived in a state home for juveniles. That was probably hard. What is he doing these days? Besides disposing of wives, that is?

SHARON. He's works for Ridgelake. He's a facilities manager.

41

BETH. Ridgelake Pharmaceuticals?

SHARON. That's right.

BETH. Do the girls know this? Does Linda?

SHARON. Yes, I think I told them he managed janitors and plumbers and maintenance staff. Why?

BETH. No—I mean do they know he works for Ridgelake?

SHARON. I don't know if I mentioned Ridgelake. Why? Does that matter?

BETH. Let me ask this. Did Ben know that you had a rat problem at the shop?

SHARON. I don't think so. I don't recall telling him about it. Kristen may have told him, I don't know. She was with me when I bought the poison. I was very careful to tell her it was poison and that she shouldn't touch it, and that she could get very sick and die if she ate it or got it on her hands. She's older now so I don't worry about that kind of thing as much as I did when she was little, but I still keep things like this out of her immediate reach.

BETH. I see. Hmm. *(SHE thinks)*

SHARON. What is it?

BETH. Nothing. It's just… *(changing the subject)* You said tomorrow is Kristen's birthday?

(SHARON nods)

I have an idea. What do you think of this?

(BETH hands SHARON her sunglasses, then takes her scarf and drapes it around SHARON's head as the curtain closes.)

(BLACKOUT)

Act 2~Scene 3

(AT RISE: STELLA., LINDA, ROSEMARY *and* BETH. have been up all night and are tired and frustrated. THEY all look "frazzled." SHARON *and* LUCILLE *are not among them.* LUCILLE *enters.)*

LUCILLE. Morning ladies. Hi Beth. Beth? Who let you stay the night? I wasn't around to fix the paperwork! *(SHE looks around)* Where's Sharon?

BETH. Now Lucille, don't get excited.

LUCILLE. She'd better be in the bathroom. Where is she?

LINDA. Now, Lucille, think of your blood pressure. Take a deep breath.

LUCILLE. I'm counting to three and then Sharon had better come out from her hiding place. One. Two....

BETH. Let me explain...

LUCILLE. Oh, no. No. Hell no! Don't tell me. You didn't. Sharon escaped. You traded places with her and snuck her out and now she's long gone and I'm accountable, right? Beth, how could you do this to me? Girl, don't you remember how good I was to you when you were here? This is what I get? This is how you thank me? They'll think I'm in on this, you know. I realize I owe you girls for all that you've done for me, but don't think I like you enough to be your new cell-mate at Black Rock. How could you do this?

STELLA. Lucille, get a grip. What are they going to do, fire you? It's a little late for that, don't you think? First of all, we have it all worked out. And if for some unfathomable reason

43

Sharon doesn't return as planned, we will be sure that everyone knows that you had nothing to do with her escape.

LUCILLE. Sure, like they'll believe you. I can't believe this. You really pushed the envelope on this one. My behind is really on the line now.

ROSEMARY. Sharon is coming back at precisely 11 a.m. You know she and Beth do have somewhat of a resemblance—Sharon just borrowed Beth's coat and scarf and glasses and they traded places for the night so that Sharon could spend time with her daughter on her birthday. She won't run, Lucille. We trust her. Meet her at the gate at eleven. She'll come dressed as Beth.

BETH. Don't be too hard on Sharon, Lucille. It was my idea.

LUCILLE. Oh, I know that! You don't have to tell me whose idea it was. I know whose idea it was. Sharon would never have come up with such a hair-brained, lame, dumb, stupid, risky...

LINDA. Okay, all right Lucille, we get the picture. Please, watch your blood pressure. I don't want you popping a hemorrhoid. We need you to be fully upright and functional.

LUCILLE. If she...

ROSEMARY. *(Firmly)* She won't. She was even reluctant to go. We had to force her. Now what did your friend say?

LUCILLE. *(Gains composure)* Beth, since you're back and already causing me trouble, you may as well go all the way.

BETH. That's what I'm here for! What do you need?

LUCILLE. Okay. Tamara—that's my private dick— rather, your private dick—Tamara has access to the usual stuff, flight schedules, airport and hotel sites, but she can't check passenger lists and even if she could—Warden is probably using an assumed name. If we can just find him we can narrow down where the funds are, and once we trace the money we can redirect it into Delval's books before he realizes it's gone. Then Tamara grabs him.

BETH. That's great. In the meantime, I'm working on the opposite strategy. I hacked into the Prison's information infrastructure and accessed the books. It appears as if Delval is in severe financial difficulty. Now, I'm working on the reverse paper trial. These data are a duplicate set of the actual records that indicate Delval's financial health. I need to retrieve that set and find out how, when, and where the funds have been transferred.

STELLA. It's our own fault, you know. We should have realized why he was so intent on finding out how we did what we did to get us in here. He even learned from our own mistakes as to how NOT to get caught. I guess I seriously underestimated the schmuck's intelligence.

ROSEMARY. Given his health, my guess is he's in a warm climate.

LINDA. Well, that leaves only one half of the hemisphere. Any other bright ideas?

ROSEMARY. In fact, I do. Lucille, does Tamara have any connections in the Caribbean?

LUCILLE. I would doubt it, but she's quite resourceful—she can get them if she has to. Why?

ROSEMARY. Remember how Warden raved about the cruise to the Caribbean we gave him and "the Missus" last year for Christmas? They had never been out of the States before, and he carried on like a little kid when he we gave him the tickets. When Warden got back it looked like he gained twenty-five pounds and his old bald head was as brown and tough as shoe leather. He showed off his photographs and strutted around like a millionaire. My guess is he started planning his great escape when he got back. He even told us the only bad thing about the entire cruise was that we had gotten his wife a ticket too. He would have preferred to go alone because of all of the single women on the ship. What a worm.

LINDA. Rosemary—you're a genius. Of course that's where the old buzzard is. It makes perfect sense. Only, this time old Mrs. Buzzard stayed home.

BETH. A lot of discrete offshore banking is done in the Virgin Islands. He probably researched it. I just can't imagine that he thought he could pull this off without our figuring it out. It's so obvious.

LUCILLE. Well, assuming Sharon returns at eleven—and if she doesn't we're all in deep trouble.... In any event, Beth needs to meet Tamara in her office to start the tracking process. I don't need to remind you about the quality of the room service menu in solitary confinement at the Black Resort and Conference Center.

STELLA. Oh Ceil, there's no need to get dramatic.

BETH. Good—that'll give me time to finish up here and get ready.

LUCILLE. You better cross your fingers and toes that Sharon's butt is back here at eleven sharp.

LINDA. You worry too much!

STELLA. I'm sure Warden also has a new identity. He probably has a new name, birth date and passport by now in order travel and funnel funds to his new accounts.

LUCILLE. That's not so hard to do if you've got the means to do it.

ROSEMARY. We know that. Beth also needs Tamara to help us investigate assumed names. We figure she'll have some inside information on this.

LINDA. It's hard to believe that no one is looking for him yet at the Department of Corrections.

LUCILLE. Oh, I just found out that Warden put in for medical leave. He's on record as having a lapa...lapa... laparoscopic cholescys-something-or-other.

LINDA. Gall bladder surgery.

STELLA.   Yeah? I'd like to remove his gall bladder with my teeth then reinsert it with a sharp object through his urethra.

LUCILLE.   Anyway, he's not AWOL officially—at least not yet.

ROSEMARY.   Damn him. He thought of everything!

BETH.   *(At computer)*   I've got it—look at this.

STELLA.   *(SHE runs to computer and reads screen)*   Great work —just what we need.

LUCILLE.   What is it?

BETH.   Telephone records from his office, cell and home phones. Give me two seconds, I'm sorting the raw data.

LINDA.   If we can determine his call patterns—incoming, outgoing, and long distance—we may be able to narrow his whereabouts even further.

STELLA.   *(Reading screen)*   This is odd. Look how many calls there were to a Mike's Gym last month. Warden never worked out a day in his life. Beth, you and Tamara may want to check that out too.

ROSEMARY.   Anybody hungry yet?

LUCILLE.   I'm starved—let's order brunch.

(BLACKOUT)

Act II~Scene 4

(SETTING: Same. Very late that evening.)

(AT RISE: **SHARON** *has returned on schedule.* **SHARON**, **LINDA** *and* **STELLA** *are sleeping.* **ROSEMARY** *is in the shower.* **LINDA** *is snoring quite audibly as the curtain rises.* **STELLA's** *cell phone rings but SHE does not answer it.)*

LINDA. *(From HER own cell)* Stella, for heaven sake, answer your phone.

STELLA. Nobody calls at this hour unless its bad news and I can't handle any more of that. Let it go to voice-mail. I'll deal with it in the morning. *(Phone stops)*

(SHE puts her pillow over her head and tries to go back to sleep. Then **LINDA**'s *cell phone rings and SHE answers.)*

LINDA. Dammit. Hello. Mrs. Bird—no, that's fine, it's not too late. I always enjoy speaking with you, too. I hope your Diverticulitis isn't giving you trouble again. No? Well, that's good. Really? Hold on a second while I get a pen. *(SHE gets pen/paper from desk.)* Who? I had no idea. Really? What does it say? Is it dated? Keep it in a safe place will you? We'll send Beth over for it in the morning. If you find anything else please let us know right away. I'm very glad you called. I know. I know. We think so, too. How are you coping? You're glad the fat bastard is gone. That's a very positive attitude, Mrs. Bird. Oh, you're quite welcome again, we're very glad you enjoyed yourself on the cruise. You're thinking about Rome next year? Yes, I agree. Italian men are very sexy. Well, Mrs. Bird, I hope

48

we can work something out. Be sure to keep in touch. Thanks again. Bye now.

> (STELLA *overhears conversation and gets up.* SHARON *does not wake up.* ROSEMARY *enters from the shower in her bathrobe with her head in a towel.*)

STELLA. What did she say? What did she say?

ROSEMARY. Who was that? Beth?

LINDA. When Beth left she paid a brief visit to Mrs. Bird and told her what we suspected about the Warden. Beth cautioned Mrs. Bird to secure their joint assets if she hadn't done so already. It turns out that they have separate bank accounts but Mrs. Bird was very grateful for our concern.

ROSEMARY. Go on...what else did she say?

LINDA. Beth also asked Mrs. Bird to look through Warden's personal effects to see if she could find anything "suspicious" like phone numbers or bank account statements or anything that may lead us to him. Beth told Mrs. Bird what we suspect about the Warden's disappearance and that we're hoping to track him down.

STELLA. And?

LINDA. Well, Mrs. Bird doesn't really care if we find him or not. Actually, she's glad to be rid of him.

STELLA. Linda! What else?

LINDA. Okay, okay—Beth asked Mrs. Bird to call us right away if she found anything at all that looked even remotely unusual, and that we would know how to reach Beth. Well, guess what Mrs. Bird found in Warden's car?

ROSEMARY. What?

LINDA. A phone message slip from their son.

STELLA. I didn't think they had children.

LINDA. He was their foster son. She said he ran away when he was a teenager because he got into some sort of trouble at school. He was almost eighteen then, so there wasn't much they could do. They tried to find him but gave up after a while. She said he was a real messed up kid.

ROSEMARY. What does that have to do with anything?

LINDA. I'm getting to that. The message said for Bird to meet him at seven o'clock on Saturday the 2nd at the SC6 Guitar Bar to discuss "retirement planning." Why would Bird want to discuss retirement planning with a foster kid he hasn't seen in years?

STELLA. This Saturday the 2nd? That's tomorrow night. *(Looks at the desk clock and realizes it is after midnight)* ...No, that's TONIGHT!

LINDA. This is the best part, guess who Bird's foster son is!

ROSEMARY. *(Sarcastically)* Tweety Bird? I don't know! Who?

LINDA. Ben Watson.

STELLA. Who's Ben Watson? *(SHE realizes)* ... Sharon's Ben Watson? He was Bird's foster child? No wonder the kid was twisted.

LINDA. Now, where in the world is the SC6 Guitar Bar. I really thought we were right about the Caribbean. Do you really think he could still be in town?

ROSEMARY. It must be a code for something.

STELLA. SC could be South Carolina. South Carolina Six? I don't get it.

ROSEMARY. SC6. South Carolina Six. Santa Clause Six. Santa Cruz Six. Saint Catherine Six. Saint Croix Six. Sandy Cofax Six?

STELLA. Isn't Koufax is spelled with a "K?"

ROSEMARY. I'm not sure.

LINDA.   Hold on—I wrote "6"—but actually she said Roman Numeral six.   That's it! Roman Numeral six is VI. St. Croix, VI—Virgin Islands. We're home!

STELLA.   There are probably over a dozen bars in St. Croix with guitar players. Even if Beth and Tamara can get a down there today they can't be at a dozen bars at seven o'clock.

ROSEMARY.   I've got it! What is the most famous "guitar" bar?

STELLA.   How would I know—I don't even know what a guitar bar is.

LINDA.   Rosemary! You're brilliant!

ROSEMARY.   Of course I am. That's what got me into trouble.

LINDA.   The Hard Rock Café! They have that giant guitar over the entrance. I think we've got them! The Hard Rock Café in St. Croix at seven tonight. I'd bet my house on it—if I still had one.

ROSEMARY.   We've got to wake Sharon. She's not going to believe this.

STELLA.   *(In a hushed tone so* SHARON *doesn't hear)* I guess it wasn't a good idea after all for Sharon to switch places with Beth. Sharon was so upset when she returned this morning. Her daughter was crying and begging her to run away. She said her daughter's friends all dumped her because her mommy is a jailbird. It broke Sharon's heart. She cried herself to sleep again.

ROSEMARY.   *(Trying to wake* SHARON*)* Sharon. Sharon, honey—guess what—you won't believe this.

(No response from SHARON*)*

STELLA.   Sharon, wake up sweetie—we have something to tell you. Sharon…Sharon?

51

> (STELLA *shakes* SHARON *to try to wake her.*
> SHARON*'s arm falls beside the bed and a bottle of*
> *pills spills onto the floor.*)

Oh my God! Linda!

    LINDA. *(Rushes to* SHARON, *takes pulse)* Call the infirmary—tell them she OD'd and to come quickly.

> (LINDA *administers CPR to* SHARON *as the*
> *curtain closes.*)

> *(CURTAIN)*

*E*ND *O*F *A*CT 2

ACT 3~Scene 1

(SETTING: A few days later)

(AT RISE: ROSEMARY, STELLA., and LINDA are packing and wrapping their belongings (curtains, pictures, memorabilia, etc) and putting them into boxes. It appears as though the day has come that they are being transferred to either Black Rock or Stone Ridge prison. THEY appear to be out of sorts. They are not in prison uniforms but are definitely "dressed down" from their usual appearances.)

ROSEMARY. What a shame. I really liked these draperies. Feel the fabric. It's such a waste.

LINDA. Maybe Lucille can use them at her place.

ROSEMARY. Remind me to ask her next time we see her.

STELLA. I guess we should ask if she'd like the television too. God knows we won't need it.

LINDA. What's going to happen to all of our things?

STELLA. I'm sure they'll keep them in storage for us until we get out. Or, maybe we should just donate everything to charity.

ROSEMARY. I never realized I could become so attached to inanimate objects.

(They continue packing in silence for a moment. Then LUCILLE enters with BETH. LUCILLE is not in her guard uniform. Instead, she wears a suit and/or is otherwise "professionally" dressed.)

STELLA. Lucille! Beth! What a surprise. Are you here for one last look around and to say goodbye?

LUCILLE. For the life of me I can't figure out why this place is so sentimental to you.

ROSEMARY. We've shared many a fond memory behind these bars. Haven't we Linda?

LINDA. Lucille, you look great. How is it going?

LUCILLE. I was nervous about everything at first, of course. But, I'm doing better now. You helped me to have confidence in myself, so I think I'll make out okay.

STELLA. Of course you will! You're going to make a terrific Warden! We are all so proud of you!

BETH. You should have seen Bird's face when Lucille, Tamara and I showed up at the bar at the Hard Rock Café with the Executive Director of the Department of Corrections and two FBI agents! He choked on the cherry in his Piña Colada. It was priceless, wasn't it Lucille?

LUCILLE. What was really priceless was when the Director offered me Warden's job right in front of him, before they cuffed and carted him and that conniving partner of his away. Delval is open for business and I'm in charge!

> (**STELLA.**, **LINDA**, **ROSEMARY** *pat* **LUCILLE**
> *on the back and wish her good luck and
> congratulations.* **SHARON** *enters from the shower*)

It's good to see you up and about young lady! You gave everyone around here quite a scare.

SHARON. I know, I'm sorry. If it weren't for Linda… *(SHE looks at* **LINDA**) Thank you. *(***LINDA** *and* **SHARON** *hug)*

LUCILLE. Hurry up now and finish packing. Pierre, the interior decorator I hired, is almost finished with your new accommodations and he is anxious for you to see his masterpiece. I took a peek—hope you don't mind. I shouldn't spoil the surprise, but you've been upgraded to private suites, each with a fully stocked mini-bar and Jacuzzi, and now you all have a fantastic view of the city skyline. Believe me, you won't miss it in here at all.

LINDA. *(To Sharon)* Chop-chop! Step it up with your packing young lady! Lucille says we don't have all day. Since she's our new Warden, when she speaks we've got to jump.

LUCILLE. Well, that's another thing I came to tell you. Linda, I'm afraid that Sharon won't be joining you.

LINDA. *(To Sharon)* Please, it's not about the snoring is it? I won't keep you up anymore! You heard what Lucille just told us. We all have private suites now. I'll even wear one of those nose gadgets if you tell me you can hear me through the walls.

SHARON. Oh no! I never minded your snoring. It actually put me to sleep some nights—kind of like ocean waves crashing onto the beach during a rough storm. No, I want to go with you! Lucille, why can't I go with them?

STELLA. Lucille, I don't understand. Sharon is one of us now. *(SHE puts a protective arm around SHARON)* Did Pierre only decorate three suites? If so, Sharon can stay with me until he finishes decorating a fourth. It's ridiculous for her to stay here while we move up to the penthouse.

LUCILLE. I'm afraid that's impossible. Sharon won't be staying here at Delval.

STELLA. *(Realizing what LUCILLE must be trying to say)* No! You can't transfer Sharon to Black Rock now! Lucille— that's inhumane!

LINDA. Lucille, really! We must protest! Sharon must stay with us at Delval and join us in the penthouse suites.

ROSEMARY. Of course she's coming with us! Lucille, please!

BETH. Just a second. You don't understand. When we explained to the Department of Corrections and the FBI about what had happened with Warden Bird and the prison's assets we also told them what we suspected about Ben Watson.

SHARON. You're kidding? What?

BETH. Ben Watson and Warden Bird never really lost touch. In fact, we think that they planned to execute—no pun intended—their individual scams and get lost in the islands together—a father and son reunion so to speak.

SHARON. Warden Bird is Ben's father? I thought Ben was an orphan.

BETH. Bird was his foster father. Ben lived with the Birds for a short time when he was in high school.

SHARON. I had no idea! Was Ben involved Warden Bird's prison scam?

BETH. Ben knew about it, that's for sure. He and daddy compared notes on scamming. Of course, Warden learned from his resident house-guests and experts here at Delval *(SHE gestures to herself,* **ROSEMARY**, **STELLA** *and* **LINDA)** and to his credit, Warden never killed anyone. Ben scams insurance companies. He murdered his last wife. In fact, we're quite sure he also killed his first one but it's doubtful that the insurance company will be able to prove it at this point. That's the one he got away with. He's not so lucky this time. The insurance company lawyers have started a massive investigation. Sharon, we're positive that the mishaps you had while you were married weren't accidents at all. You were the lucky one.

SHARON. My God! You mean Ben actually poisoned Diane? How?

BETH. Remember when I asked if Linda knew that Ben works for Ridgelake Pharmaceuticals? If she knew she would have made the connection right away. Ridgelake manufactures Warfarin, an anticoagulant. It's more or less the same chemical compound that is in rat poison. Since Ben was the Facilities Manager he had access to the entire building—even the research labs and the manufacturing plant. We checked with Ridgelake's Security Department and they confirmed that a small quantity of Warfarin had been reported as stolen on the morning of Diane's death. They were in the process of conducting an internal investigation. I'm sure it was just a matter of time before they reached the conclusion that we did. Still, it would have been difficult, if not impossible, for them to prove with only circumstantial evidence.

SHARON. This is unbelievable!

ROSEMARY. Also, Beth traced a number of calls that Bird made to Mike's Gym last month.

SHARON. That's where Ben works out.

BETH. Yes, we figured that out when I hacked into the gym's membership lists.

LUCILLE. Ben Watson and Warden Bird are having a reunion all right—but at Black Rock Federal Penitentiary—not in the Virgin Islands. Sharon...here are your release papers. You are free to go.

> (**SHARON** *gives a shriek of joy and starts crying and takes out a tissue.*)

LINDA. Oh, not again! Go. Go! Go on and get out of here.

SHARON. Oh, thank you, thank you all. I'll miss you all so much. I can't thank you enough for everything you've done for me.

LUCILLE. Come on now. Let's hurry...you've got a daughter upstairs who is very anxious to see you.

SHARON. Kristen's here?

LUCILLE. She's playing a game on the computer in my office—don't worry—I've got a very responsible guard babysitting. She's fine.

> (*THEY give hugs and kisses goodbye all around—*
> **SHARON** *and* **LUCILLE** *leave*)

ROSEMARY. Well, the only thing that could make this day more perfect is if you were back with us, Beth.

BETH. Well, you got your wish—I'm back!

LINDA. What do you mean? They didn't nail you for hacking into the prison's computer system did they? I mean, after all—you saved their assets and the prison doesn't have to close. Delval is in perfect financial health.

BETH. You're right. And I'm not being prosecuted. In fact, the Department is so grateful to all of us that they offered me the position as head of Information Technology. My first priority is to ensure security for the prison's information systems. The best part is, I can come and go as I please and, stay with you whenever and for as long as I want.

STELLA. That's fantastic!

BETH. That's not all. Lucille and I told everyone that the three of you were really the driving force behind the Warden and Ben Watson's capture—and that all I really did was follow your instructions and direction.

ROSEMARY. Beth you're too modest. You always put others first.

BETH. So, the Department convened a special Review Board that decided to substantially reduce your remaining sentences. Stella and Rose—you'll both be out in one year.

(STELLA *and* LINDA *shriek with joy and hug each other.*)

Linda! You're out in six months!

LINDA. Six months! Yahoo! Hey, maybe I'll give Mrs. Bird a call and see if she wants a travel companion in Rome. I wouldn't mind checking out those sexy Italian men myself!

ROSEMARY. I know! Let's all plan to meet in Rome next year when Stella and I are released. Lucille and Sharon, too! A Roman reunion of the Delval Divas! Those Italian men won't know what hit them!

STELLA.   This calls for a celebration!   *(SHE unpacks a bottle of champagne from one of the boxes)*   Rosemary! Unpack the crystal!

(**FINAL CURTAIN**)

* * *

MUSIC USE NOTE

Licensees are solely responsible for obtaining formal written permission from copyright owners to use copyrighted music in the performance of this play and are strongly cautioned to do so. If no such permission is obtained by the licensee, then the licensee must use only original music that the licensee owns and controls. Licensees are solely responsible and liable for all music clearances and shall indemnify the copyright owners of the play(s) and their licensing agent, Samuel French, against any costs, expenses, losses and liabilities arising from the use of music by licensees. Please contact the appropriate music licensing authority in your territory for the rights to any incidental music.

IMPORTANT BILLING AND CREDIT REQUIREMENTS

If you have obtained performance rights to this title, please refer to your licensing agreement for important billing and credit requirements.